The World in an Eye

The World in an Eye

Maroula Blades

Chapeltown Books

British Library Cataloguing in Publication Data

A Record of this Publication is available from the British Library

ISBN 978-1-910542-56-9

This edition published 2020 by Chapeltown Books
Manchester, England

Contents

Introduction

The World in an Eye is the result of years of observation, researching, empathising, listening to and living with the powerless. These diversifying flash fiction stories solicit the *call* to activism by certifying, raising, and supporting the fervent voices of the unheard. These characters become a collective, rallying together to claim the air they breathe and the ground they stand on. They vocalize truths: we are and will always be here, so deal with us with equal measure as you do for the better-offs in society.

A certain discomfort might be felt when reading *The World in an Eye*. A disturbed silence may ensue that pricks sensibilities. The objective of these stories is not to generate pity or to ear bash the reader; it is to find camaraderie.

Sunlight will swathe all of us as we levitate to the world's stage where dialogue and reflection rules the day.

Lives on Recycled Paper

A Letter for the Mayor

'Hello, Ms. Ronin, how are you?'

'Who wants to know?'

'My name is Dorothy. I'm the senior journalist and editor for my college magazine.'

'Who sent you?'

'Your son is a friend of mine; we bowl together on Sundays.'

'Ah, yes, I remember you called last week.'

'I did. You told me to meet you here at two o'clock. I'm here. Why meet in the park?'

'I had no money to take a bus, so I walked from home. It's okay, the park is joyful in the summer, look at these silver birches.'

'You're right. What's that you're carrying?'

'A letter for the Mayor written on recycled paper. I made the paper in the Japanese arts and crafts course at the adult education centre.'

'Oh!'

'I'm learning Japanese too.'

'Japanese, that must be difficult.'

'It is, but only because of my age; after fifty, the brains cells aren't so with it.'

'I understand. So, that letter you're holding, what's in it?'

'My family's story.'

'Would you like to share it with me?'

'Well, the bad luck moved in during 2014. Someone flung a Molotov cocktail at our front door where it exploded into flames. The fire raced through the apartment, killed my daughter, Belinda. She was twelve years old. We lost everything.'

'Would you like a tissue, Ms. Ronin?'

'No, thanks, I've got one.'

'Marvin's a good boy. While studying, he also worked at the off-licence in the evenings. He was saving to buy us new furniture.'

'Did everything burn?'

'Yes, everything went up in flames, except the stove and our old metal bathtub. We bought cardboard furniture called Damaris.'

'I've heard of it. The tables and chairs are practical and solid. Can you tell me what happened to Marvin? I heard he got arrested for stealing, spent time in jail, and now he's in the hospital with serious injuries.'

'Marvin wasn't stealing anything.'

'Okay, go on, Ms. Ronin.'

'He and his friend Mikey found a used sofa on the pavement. Mikey told me what Marvin said on that day, *it's tatty, but Mum will appreciate it.*'

'And so they picked it up, Ms. Ronin?'

'Yes.'

'And then what happened?'

'The owner of the sofa placed it on the street because pest controllers were fumigating his apartment. He called them in because of a spider infestation.'

'I hate spiders, Ms. Ronin, yuck.'

'Baby spiders hatched on his guava fruits; they sat in a ceramic bowl on top of the fridge. They kept a few babies and took them to the aquarium where they have arachnid tanks.'

'You're kidding?'

'No, anyway, the owner of the sofa, a white man, saw the boys walking down the road carrying his possession. He called the police.'

'Because of a sofa, Ms. Ronin?'

'Yes. A policeman shouted as he shot two bullets in the direction of the boys.'

'Sounds awful.'

'Marvin said in court that first bullet whistled passed his ear. And the second one, he felt clipping the air by his right knee; he wore board shorts that day. The boys froze and dropped the sofa.'

'I'm not surprised.'

'Marvin was thrown in jail for theft; he got a six-month sentence. The first night in his shared cell two prisoners sexually assaulted him. He lost his mind for a while. A prison warden transferred him to a sanatorium where he was attacked.'

'I'm so sorry to hear that, Ms. Ronin. Marvin's a great guy. How he's suffered, it's so unfair.'

'As I said before, I made the paper this letter is written on in my art course. The wood came from a local oak tree. Fungus infected four of its boughs, they were sawn off. I was happy to hear an arborist saved the tree.'

'A local tree, you say, Ms. Ronin?'

'Yes. Mr. Ainara, my art teacher, found the boughs on the ground in this park and decided to make good use of them. He said, "Trees have souls, the boughs shouldn't be laid to waste like that".'

'Mr. Ainara sounds like a wise man.'

'Yes, he is. This paper literally comes from this here soil. Its soul has witnessed the goings and comings of this area for three hundred years.'

'Awesome. Come, I'll walk you to the Town Hall.'

'Thanks, Dorothy, but it's only five minutes away.'

'I know. Let's walk and talk, Ms. Ronin.'

'This letter holds Marvin's testimony as well as mine. My lovely boy now lies in hospital with a broken collarbone, three cracked ribs, and a ruptured spleen. No one has been arrested for attacking him.'

'Goodness. I'm sorry, I wish I could do more.'

'Dorothy, at least you care and you're interested in getting to the truth.'

'Can I ask you one more question?'

'Go ahead.'

'You have a different surname to your son, why's that?'

'After all the bad things happened, I couldn't live with the name Jackson anymore, it's a slave name. I researched it on the internet at a family history website. The information made me sick, it made me feel lonely. I needed a stronger name to fortify my spirit and to strengthen my focus.'

'Was it difficult changing your name?'

'No. I've been a divorcee for ten years, so, I was able to change it. Ronin is a Japanese name. It means a vagrant samurai without a master.'

'Wow.'

'Here we are, Ms. Ronin, in front of the town hall where I hope you'll be able to have a consultation with the Mayor.'

'Me too.'

'Good luck! Thanks for sharing your's and Marvin's story. Bye.'

'You're welcome, Dorothy.'

'Don't mind me, I'm still recording.'

'Okay.'

'Ms. Ronin ascends the steps of the town hall. Her steps are weary, but her head is high. She's clutching a letter made from recycled paper. She has calligraphed her heart and that of her son's, Marvin, on the page in Indian deep red ink.'

Waiting

I can almost pick up his dreams in the throes of a mad world. Cigarette-butts lay frozen near his blue rubber clogs. His eyes roll in their sockets. His eyes reflect his panic as a yellow lorry, loaded with full-fat dairy products, tears up the road, rumbling, trying to catch the amber traffic light before the red switches on above the two-lane street. It stops in front of me, a huge print on the side of its metal frame is one of a picturesque landscape; a picnic and fat, hairy cows grazing in an open field.

On a patch of freshly cut wheat, a starched red gingham tablecloth with perfect edges sprawls out. A large slab of butter with its golden wrapper folded neatly down on a porcelain dish brings a slight smile to my face. From the crusty brown rolls, thin curls of steam rise. I imagine the delicious smell and feel the baked warmth, heat from another dimension.

Beside the plate is an outsized bottle of milk with a thick cream layer at the bottleneck. A bunch of sunny daffodils show off their full beauty, fanning out on the cloth, mirroring a half sun. A minute later, the scene is lost up the road.

As crowds bustle past tormented by the weather, an image of a compass comes to mind. Umbrellas and hats want to make a quick getaway. In this fume-logged city air, a broad lamp-post props me up, as I hug myself in my nylon puffer-jacket with a broken zip against the chilly wind that shoves empty beer cans and bottles into the gutter. The bruised cans clank on their journey southwards. A pungent odour lifts with a cause from the shoeless body, sleeping behind me on the frost-lit bench. It is odd that in his state one can almost be invisible.

The queue for the bus is getting longer; most eyes are fixed on the tarmac. In the waiting, the feeling of cold inches up the feet to the calves that tense to hold their ground. A heavily pregnant woman looks towards the bench. Out of the corner of my eye I see her shrugging shoulders, as if to say, *such is life!* She waddles towards me, positioning her body on the other side of the lamp-post where she drops shopping bags to the ground, heaves a breath and eases herself slowly, back first, to the post.

Dusk falls at a snail's pace. The feeling of cold shifts, pelting up sleeves, stealing body heat; my teeth chatter. We are both in need of something, as is the thin life-bitten man, shivering in sleep.

The Papaya Stall

Witness:

Gunfire coloured his shirt; mournful-red seeped through the sharp white garment. A buttonhole strained open with the top button at the neck; folds of chubby flesh hung over the starched collar. Time slowed; a crippling pace. It was bitter and windy. A yellow crane in the distance struggled with a huge concrete slab; it slipped, thick wires held.

The tread of heavy boots and the piercing sound of sirens filled the marketplace. I bolted to a papaya stall; one fruit was halved, a black seed cluster sat in a hollow of deep orange-red. Under the grassy cover, I crouched, hands cupping ears. Dissonant chimes from the Holy Mother Church vibrated through fingers. More shots walloped the air.

A walkie-talkie screeched, 'Paramedics are on the way.'

I peeped out of the brushy keyhole-weave in the cloth. Orange-clad figures raced with a gurney. With a caring touch, they lifted the heavy male body. The head rolled to the side, my side.

I screamed. It was Uncle Leonard with a bunch of leafy bio carrots near his right hand. I crawled to him; I could not walk. Nearby, packed tight in an unzipped death bag, Aunt Cecilia lay with a clean bullet wound between her eyes and one shot in the left kneecap. Her attire was oddly new. She wore pearly-snakeskin stilettos, a black leather miniskirt, and a stretch-fit, silver halter top. Crimson lip gloss smeared across her smooth face.

My mind flashed back to last Sunday's service. Aunt Cecilia always sat in the same spot for years, the front pew in the church. She looked like summer, wearing a beautiful honeysuckle toned dress with a matching billycan large brim hat. She worshipped in tongues. Her well trained contralto sung heartfelt spirituals that ministered to the congregation. Old women cried that day.

I noticed, as she lay there, swamped by synthetic black cloth, a fresh purple-blue bruise rose from her chin. Her mouth stood open; a front tooth was chipped. Blood oozed out from black fishnet stockings. I touched her face; it was still warm.

Crutches

I felt light on my eyelids, eyes blinked open.

A man stood over me, shouting, 'You've killed them!'

A firefighter led the wild-looking man away, covering his shoulders with a grim blanket. Pain soared, rushing up my body. I was lying on the pavement where the smell of tar soaked the air. Nausea filled my throat. Blood ran into my sight. Someone panted heavily beside me, but I couldn't turn to see who was there. Feet scurried, voices rumbled and then darkness fell.

The surgeon said I was lucky to be alive. I looked down the sterile bedding; my eyes fell upon a space where my right leg should have been. Brenda, my wife stroked my cheek. I was glad Tillie, our daughter, wasn't with her.

I yelled, 'Where is it?'

'Shush, darling, you need to rest. Everything will be fine.'

I swayed between white light and shadows until finally Brenda and the room were fixed. She held my hand; her grip was hot and clammy.

'It's going to be all right,' she whispered.

She lied. In her eyes, I saw pain and the worry of an uncertain future with an invalid, clouding and fracturing her mind. What had happened? I tried to piece together fragments of that fatal Monday morning. The mist filtered up from memory and a white car with dimmed headlamps. I heard quiet talk of an inquiry into two deaths, from a police officer and a doctor standing in a corner of the room.

Weeks passed. I was still none the wiser. What had happened? After a four-month spell in the hospital, I was released. At home, I lay, staring into the stillness of my room. Finally, I plucked up courage to venture outside the house. Neighbours with pity glazing their eyes said fleeting hellos, as Brenda wheeled me to the park where ducks swam in the lake's stagnant water. My left leg quivered. Muscles that were once taut, hung in sagging skin.

I missed playing squash with my friend Brian. Brian had visited me only twice. He left after fifteen minutes with a flimsy excuse dug deep in his throat; it kept on echoing at my bedside.

'I've got loads of work to do, must dash.'

Nothing made sense anymore. What lies behind the power of friendship and what principle binds it? In Brian's case, it was flaky, like pastry.

An important letter arrived, registered post. Brenda read it aloud. The notice stated that the premature deaths of a toddler aged three, named Sandra, and her mother, Joyce Lang, were caused by accident, due to poor visibility. There will be no further investigation.

Brenda flapped her hands like flags and wept. She baked a cream sponge cake that evening.

I was ungrateful, nothing mattered that used to matter. Brenda soon became impatient with my lack of commitment in coming to terms with my disability. I threw cups of tea, bowls of soup and full plates of food at the walls. Food stuck to the pastel-coloured wallpaper like putrid flowers. The bedroom resembled a rubbish tip and stunk like one too. Maggots wriggled in the waste. I watched their white ribbed bodies multiply on a rotten apple core.

Brenda informed my doctor, who prescribed antidepressants and mood enhancers, but I still felt anxious. Bug exterminators were called in to fumigate the place, they looked like astronauts.

My body felt like a can of worms ready to burst as warm water touched skin. From my groin, I gave birth to slugs, still attached to the area by their tails; they surged with the bathwater. I smashed the snake-like head of the shower appliance against the enamel bathtub, screamed as the pink tube slithered into the water near my foot; a huge worm knotted around my ankle. The doctor said I was exhibiting bipolar-like symptoms, but it was too early for a complete diagnosis.

Brenda bought me a journal where I should record my feelings.

What a load of rubbish, I thought, as she handed me the book as if it were a prized treasure. *I don't need a bloody book; I want my leg back.*

One night, I overheard Tillie saying, 'Mum, I'm afraid of Dad. He's changed so much since the accident.'

'I know, dear, he needs to take his medicine regularly, but he doesn't.'

Later that year, my wife filed for a divorce. Who could blame her? I was an altered man.

Moving into a urine-smelling hostel with other men with mental and physical disabilities took me to the next phase, one that ended in making daily trips to the supermarket to buy cheap bottles of booze. At night, I screamed aloud.

A re-occurring dream haunts, *a car is swerving as I cross a road painted with white stripes. A child crashes through the windshield. A dark-haired woman sits pinned, screaming behind the steering wheel with a gash in her skull. Blood spews. I run towards the crash site. A signpost is on the ground. More headlights zigzag, running across my shadow and then something clips the side of me. The next minute, I am lying next to a woman. She is wheezing. The panting suddenly stops.*

Fleabites pock my skin. My leg is a permanent feverish itch and sting. The landlord sends me letters of complaints. His last note is written in capitals, "SHAPE UP OR GET OUT!"

I move out onto the streets where space is vast and most people move quickly away from me. It's okay. I know what I must look like to the rest of the world with crusty scabs covering my face, walking on two odd-coloured crutches, with plastic bags full of soiled clothes, photos and diaries stretching from the Day-Glo-pink and turquoise handgrips. The pee-stained jogging suit I am wearing is scary, but I do not care.

Things cling to my Rasputin-like beard. At times, I sense a creeping sensation between the matted hairs. The flattened cigarette butt that I have just found at a bus stop will comfort me until I find the next one. It is a struggle, balancing on crutches, bending down to reach for discarded things. My metal cup, attached to a cord, slipped and rolled off into a muck-filled gutter last week. A woman with a squirming face picked it up with a handful of tissues and gave it to me. I nodded my thanks.

The scuffed, tan brogue I wear on my only foot needs resoling. I used to love the brogues; they were on my feet at my wedding. The right shoe I kept; it looks almost new. Most days, I hobble along come rain, sun, or snow, eyes forever fixed down. I don't drink anymore; it involved begging like a scraggy dog waiting for a half-chewed morsel that was a long time coming. Traffic scares me. I hide behind trees at peak times to avoid the rush of noise charging through my head. Hands tremble. Faintness splashes the mind with balls of light.

A stranger's voice cuts through the base of memory, 'You've killed them!'

Words pound like a sledgehammer, tears roll.

Last week, I visited that street. There were new traffic lights.

At the base of the pedestrian signpost, I placed wild flowers in my mint brown brogue, the one from the missing foot.

Dripping Teeth

She wanted to fight scorpion-style in the gridlock. Through the cold lens of life, I watched mad streaks of lemon-fire burst in her eyes. She was buoyant in black gym clothes, as she jabbed the air and skipped an imaginary rope on the fourth-floor landing of our building. Planks of wood from a king-sized bed frame criss-crossed the landing; male toiletries were on the steps together with a shiny pair of size ten dress shoes and a three-piece suit. I tripped on a grey shoe.

It was about 1.00 a.m. on a Saturday. I had bolted up two flights of stairs to see what the commotion was about.

I thought someone was trying to break into a flat, the din sounded like a door being kicked in.

The neighbour opposite Ms. Scorpion stood with her large frame positioned in front of a freshly scratched door; the deep cuts in wood and paint ran from top to bottom. The neighbour only wore an off-white T-shirt and unseemly underwear; varicose veins plagued her stout lower body.

Surprised by the scene, I cupped my mouth. Ms. Scorpion screamed and hissed in a language unknown to my tongue, Russian. I ran towards them as Ms. Scorpion lifted a dustpan by its wide body and cracked a forceful blow with the red handle on the forehead of her rival. Immediately, a bump grew and blood trickled out of the wound. The browbeaten woman cradled her alopecia skull, rocking in pain.

More words spat from Ms. Scorpion's mouth, as she elbowed my solar plexus. Winded, I fell with a thud against the whitewashed coffin-cold wall and slid to the ground. She threw down the dustpan; it bounced twice and then it took a wayward path down the stairs.

All of a sudden, Ms. Scorpion whipped out her dripping dentures and with the index finger of the other hand, she poked her chin, as if to provoke a blow from her adversary. Her foe recoiled. Thin lips disappeared quickly in a gum-rotten mouth. The stale plastic teeth dribbleded clear-coloured globules onto the brown linoleum floor near my feet. Without a second to waste, I drew them in. Halitosis wriggled like a demon in the stairwell.

I took a eucalyptus-scented tissue from the pocket of my towelling dressing gown and placed it over my nose. Aches pulsated just below my ribcage; breath slowly returned.

Ms. Scorpion screamed in cyclic rhythms; a war chant, her inflamed uvula danced at the back of her throat. The neighbour swore, slamming her door shut.

I shivered; goose bumps ran the length of my arms. The chant echoed and shook the whole neighbourhood awake until the law enforcement officers arrived, thundering up the stairs to subdue the fracas. They arrested the toothless woman, but before handcuffing her wrists, she shoved the stale dentures back into the orifice, fixing the dripping teeth to worn gums with a dust-encrusted hand. She winced.

As she was led away, she snarled in my direction. Down the stairwell, she screamed and kicked, no one understood her cries.

Looking for Polly

It happened last Saturday night after going to Nick's 30th birthday bash. Feeling nauseous at 1.00 a.m., I staggered to catch the last train home. While sitting on a platform bench, my eyes rolled backwards and the lids shut tight. Ten minutes later, and on time too, the train screeched to a halt. Shaking the sleep from my body, I scrambled into an empty carriage, where I rested for half an hour.

I arrived home at 2.15 a.m. While searching for my keys, I realised Polly, my *iPhone* was gone. A pickpocket must have taken her while I napped in the station. The muscles around my jaw tightened. Opening the door, feeling devastated by the loss, I kicked off my brogues; they flew and knocked a Paul Gauguin print *Riders on the Beach* (1902), off the wall. Wood and glass shards crusted the parquet floor.

Boiling inside on the brink of exploding, I went into the kitchen to make coffee. After gulping down half a litre of hot black fluid, I cracked my knuckles and switched on the computer. Thank God, I had previously configured Polly so that if she was stolen, I could lock her and erase her memory. I initiated the trace function. Then I fell back on plump pillows and slept.

The following day, I woke at 9.00 a.m. Still dressed in my smart, but crumpled tan linen suit, I went to shower. The water refreshed me. Life slowly crept from my puny toes to my mushy brain. Then it dawned on me, Polly was missing, and how much that meant.

I had just met Stella at Nick's party, a lovely five-foot two brunette with an intelligent face, who I would hate to give up. Getting her number took me ages. I wrangled with all the chat up lines known to man until the petite beauty finally succumbed to my masculine undying powers that glimmered in the light of the beeswax candles.

After showering, armed with a mug of coffee and a menthol cigarette, I went to examine the trace function. Bingo! Polly was found. The police were informed and filed a report. Even though the trace function is accurate, the radius was too large to probe. I turned off the computer and sulked. In my purple, samurai-like dressing gown I munched low-fat crisps and repeatedly switched TV channels.

At 4.30 p.m. I decided to go for a jog, but not before checking the trace function again. Polly had not journeyed on. A park was located in the trace radius.

A good place to run, I thought, *maybe the thief dumped Polly in a bin.*

The idea of Polly lying in waste made me wince. I tucked rubber gloves into the waist of my jogging pants – that looked cool. They would come in handy to sift through the filth in the rubbish bins.

The weather was warm and ferns danced in the dry August breeze. I started to feel better, thinking about the toxins from the previous night's bash easing their way out in beads through the skin. I put on the rubber gloves. As I jogged, every rubbish bin was inspected, but with no luck. I was beginning to think Polly was lost forever and felt crushed. I stopped to sip mineral water and wiped the perspiration from my brow. My eyes scoured the area. Across the road sat a huge skip filled with broken tiles and cement.

Worry pierced me right between the eyes.

Polly would be cracked and scratched, ruined in that thing, I thought.

I sprinted over to the container, jumped in and rummaged around like a maniac. I was up to my knees in flaky rubbish. Sadly, my gloves were not primrose yellow anymore, but moth brown. I heard a faint cry or was it a meow? Was it a kitten in a box somewhere amongst the debris? There was no sight of Polly, but there was a new-born with its umbilical cord still attached in a shoebox, lying on a stained dishcloth.

'Good God, you sad poor thing.'

I picked the tiny boy up; flaky black blood covered him. He was shaking and partially blue. My T-shirt came in handy for wrapping him.

It would be great to have my Polly now, I thought.

In despair, I threw a lump of cement to the ground; it hopped three times on the tarmac. I looked to the murky skies for a clue. As my tearful eyes wandered, they fell on a second-hand mobile store next door to a small bakery on the corner of the street. I sprung out of the skip, bolted to the bakery where a friendly-looking plump lady came to my aid.

'I found this baby across the road in the skip.'

'Goodness, the poor little love.'

'Please call the police and welfare department too.'

'Sure. How can anyone be so awful? Just leaving him like that.'

The baker sang a nursery rhyme. As she rocked the baby in one arm and with the other, she dialled a number with the receiver wedged between her neck and shoulder.

'The police are coming.'

'Great. I've got things to do. Can I leave the little mite with you?'

'Yes, but don't you…?'

'You know the story. Just tell the police. Here's my name and address. If they want me to corroborate it, they'll contact me.'

'Okay. Ah, look the small one is sleeping.'

At home, I checked the computer again. Polly was still in the same position, perhaps she was in the second-hand shop. I called Dennis, a good friend to accompany me to the store on Monday morning and asked him to bring his laptop. The police were informed of my hunch; they would meet us outside the store armed to the hilt with batons and Tasers.

Dennis arrived at 9.30 a.m. He drove us to the location in his beaten-up blue Volvo. Normally, I would not be seen dead in such a vehicle, but I was desperate. As we parked, two police officers approached us from the opposite direction. I signalled to them, raising a crisp-white cotton arm. Dennis opened his laptop while walking and activated the secure dialling ring in Polly; she would soon chime for two minutes. We entered the shabby store.

The shopkeeper looked nervous and stuttered his hello. I wrote down my stolen *iPhone* model on a slip of paper and handed it to him. A police officer jotted down notes in a slim black pad that had seen better days. Dennis hit the enter button to initiate the ring. I heard Polly singing the blues from somewhere in the back.

I shouted, 'I hear her. That's my Polly, I know it is.'

Both police officers frowned.

The shopkeeper spoke fast. He said he had bought such a model from a down-at-the-mouth guy who was waiting outside the shop when he arrived in the morning. He gave him ten pounds.

Stingy cretin, I thought.

He continued adding, 'He didn't want a receipt. He took off sharply. I made a note of the sale, look!'

He was addressing one of the officers, holding up a blotchy receipt book. The shopkeeper left us for a moment.

One officer turned to me and said, 'I know you.'

'You do?'

'I recognise your name from a recent report sheet. You're the one who rescued baby John, aren't you?'

'Baby John?'

'The new-born.'

'Oh, yeah, the baby. Yes, I found him over there in that dirty skip while searching for my phone. He was in a shoebox, surrounded by crack tiles and dead mice.'

'You got more than you bargained for, aye?'

'I certainly did.'

'Laura Parkers, the baker, named the baby. She wants to adopt him. She and her husband haven't any children, but always wanted one.'

'Oh, that's nice.'

'Totally.'

'My life's far too busy for a kid, what with working at the bank, playing tennis twice a week and brunching with friends on the weekend.'

'Everyone to their own.'

'Look at the state of the world, anyway, you'd have to be crazy to bring one into it.'

The storekeeper returned holding Polly in an ink-stained hand. She was still singing her little heart out; bless her. He handed Polly over.

I grabbed her, wiped her with a eucalyptus oil impregnated tissue and then kissed her.

'Hi, baby, I'm taking you home,' I whispered.

The officer who spoke to me scowled and barked, 'I see you have your phone. You care for it like it's human.'

'You're damn right, she's my life. Come, Dennis, I want to go home. I've time for two interactive games before bruncheon. Bye.'

We Owe It to You

For Rosa Parks

It takes a movement to bring about change in dry infinity or, some may say, the lack of one. Your tired legs could stand no longer. In "no man's land" you sat, clasping painkillers on your lap. A colourless rider stood in the aisle.

The bus driver's coarse voice punched the air with, 'All right, you niggers. I want those seats.'

Your quiet 'No,' a distended cloud, rained on Montgomery, Alabama 1955 where the eyes of whiteness stalked the streets. Phantoms with spike tongues ran, flaunting coshes to thrash "darkie's flesh". The Jim Crow law marched without a curfew.

A paper chase settled on the lawn of the Supreme Court. The puzzle of names screamed as they came together, counted. Even the ghosts cut their nooses from budding Memorial Trees, faces with crooked lips, gouged out eyes and abysses where their manhood should be, rallied.

The wind morphed battered features, floating on the Mississippi River, a painful exhibit of fathers, brothers and youths. Snagged, waterlogged bodies defiantly rose from the river root, some with bobby socks and plaits, and others who had once the form of gazelles faced the sun, anaemic and bloated.

Black peeled itself away from the backs of mirrors, a transparent happening. No excuses not to see through the window. It took 382 days.

The mandate: *Alabama's bus segregation laws unconstitutional.*

You became our planet, the sun for Black folk to turn to. Swarthy necks grew out from your orbit, gravitating towards freedom's light. *Onward Christian Soldiers*, armed with a protest, a pillar of blackness with an aim as sharp as a pickaxe. Soulful voices echoed for miles out of the ghettos, over moonscapes and down through the tree-lined suburbs.

A future ran straight into our hearts, designed like a main road.

The stone which fell, is still falling, your word freed it, but it still feels the burn of repression in the free fall. Your titanium smile is etched in the core, a fire of light in the dark, a flickering universe of hope that tomorrow will be brighter, wiser and full of release.

For the Love of Money

It wasn't much, but it was home. For days we, the tenants, and members of our community like Mrs. Wrench, a primary teacher, Mr. Lowry, the street baker, Mr. Hall, the preacher, and others, stood silent with linked arms. We thought this was an impenetrable formation around our crumbling three storey home of sixteen leaking, mouldy apartments.

The enormous crane with its pear-shaped wrecking ball and steel chain, threatened at a short distance away. Red-necked city developers urged, menaced, and called the police who made on-the-spot arrests.

At the time two single women held their illegitimate toddlers in their arms. Tardy welfare workers came in, took the kids and packed them like suitcases in the back of a rusty grey Volvo. They were just doing their job, but aren't carers meant to care, to feel and empathise with the poor circumstances that the deprived experienced? Instead, irritation crumpled their faces, as the mothers struggled in vain to hold tight to their babes.

Our protest fizzed out to the sound of gushing water from hoses that sprayed our bodies with the ripping power of talons. Tenants took to flight, running to their cold-water flats to take as many belongings as possible. Elderly Mr. Lennox strapped a tired-looking mattress on his hunched back. He set off to hobble the length of the street to the corner where his childhood friend, Mrs. Blake, waited. Mrs. Blake, a widow and now homeless, had set up camp with a pitcher of lemonade. The childhood friends grew up here and wanted to live out their last days in the area even if that meant living on the street amid the waste and rats.

From my flat, I came out tearful and lost a shoe down the stairwell. I watched the shoe fumble the concrete on its descent. Out on the curb, mean machines with stony faces wore shiny badges, uniforms, and holstered pistols. Into the city-grey the new homeless walked, along the streets where pimps and prostitutes called out from flashy convertibles, trying to entice the young to pay a coin for a ride to an unknown destination.

Corrupt taxi men and fossil-like oldies were also on the move, or should I write prowl, in souped-up automobiles. They acted like treacle wouldn't ooze from their lips, while asking, 'Are you lost? Need a lift home? Looks like I'm going in your direction.'

Libby, a young mother who loved to party, arrived home to find no home. Dressed in club-clothes, she sat in her red leather mini on a patch of dry earth. Her mother had left earlier in the morning with her grandson to the other side of town. Tear-stained, Libby stretched out, looked skyward and mouthed words lighter than whispers. I took Libby's hand and hauled her to her feet. As we walked, fancy cars and taxis tooted horns and randy old men tried to disguise their intentions with polite renditions of 1950's talk.

We dragged our feet; they hurt while walking the hill. Atop the hillock, we witnessed the final swing of the crane's steel ball, and the handshakes between city developers, police and wealthy city folk. Above them in a cab, hundreds of feet above the worksite, the crane's cab-operator did a thumbs up sign. He was ablaze with the satisfaction of wreaking havoc.

For adoption, we are too old, but not old for the filth and swank of the city's keen-eyed sex-predators. These low-life hustlers saw an expanding *capital* before their red-streaked eyes. Vigilant, we trekked, ignoring the low calls from lanky shadows in dingy corners.

On the following scorching day, we continued to walk, huddled together down a never-ending road.

What's It All For?

'Hi Caroline, it's Teresa. I've burnt my hair. I didn't pin it back while lighting the fire last night. A chunk of wood spluttered; I ran and cushioned the flames with a wet towel.'

'Really!'

'I feel so depressed. I looked into a mirror; I saw a huge bare patch. I then took my Dad's clippers and shaved the rest off.'

'You're kidding, aren't you?'

I had to get a grip of myself.

'It's okay, Sweetie, it will grow back.'

'I've bought a wig from the Afro-shop called *Carmen*. I've always wanted to try a perm. The wig doesn't suit me though, but I'm too afraid to show my prickly skull. I don't know what to do.'

'Do some yoga; you'll feel a lot calmer if you do. Remember that CD I gave you *Finding The Inner You?* Give it a go. I'll be there in an hour, okay?'

'You should have seen me this morning. I wore a pair of thick grey tights on my head. I wrapped the legs around like a turban. I didn't realise at the time a holey foot had aired itself on the bus. Everyone was laughing, even I giggled. When I arrived at the Afro-shop, I realised the joke was on me. I broke down and cried. The shop assistant brought me a cup of tea.'

'Try not to worry; it will all turn out fine. Hair grows back, you know.'

Teresa constantly moaned about her looks and weight. I suggested vegetable drinks and yoga. She would begin the new regime well but capitulate when signs of progress showed.

'What's it all for?' asked Teresa. 'No one wants me anyway.'

'It's for you, Sweetie. You've such a pretty face.'

At home, Teresa sat in the shadows, prodding her tummy while eating custard doughnuts. She always sat facing a blank wall at 10.00 p.m. Teresa watched the evening's traffic project light beams on the cold surface. Sometimes she would trace the moving lights with a finger, hoping to absorb some warmth. I caught her many times doing this when we lived together while attending college. Every day, Teresa felt unloved and uneasy in the world. It was a shame to see her so, I felt for her. I wanted to give her a big, warm hug. But decided against it, not wanting to embarrass her and myself in the process.

On 24th December 2011, she drove her car to a wood and crashed it into a tree. The blue car paint still spots the bark.

I pinned a note to the tree on Christmas Day. It read:

I miss you, Teresa, so much. You were a perfect being. I'm sorry, I didn't have the courage to tell you 'I love you.'

Punch Drunk

'I need a bloody drink!' Lydia said, 'I don't know what to do, Sis. My boss, the bloody jerk, keeps putting his white, floppy hands on my backside.'

'Really, that's the pits! Come in and flip your shoes off while I pour a couple of rum and blacks. It's the turquoise peddle-pushers you're using, Lydia, they're showing too much lineage.'

'So, what, I still think he should keep his flaming hands to himself. I might file a complaint next week for sexual harassment. He's really got my back up, always touching my *mumf* like it's up for grabs.'

Lydia gulps four mouthfuls of potent brew and crushes ice with her molars.

'What makes it worse, Sis, he's already got one bloody leg in the grave and the other has a round of gout plaguing it.'

'He sounds like a bloody nightmare to me, Lyd. I think I need another stiff drink. I feel like belting him too with an ice-filled sock around the head shouting, "hello, is there anyone at home?" I know it's hard work at the office with all those men. Testosterone is always a summer problem.'

I pour ample amounts of white rum into long, thin glasses. *It's after 7.00 p.m. Five cl are more fitting than two cl at this time of day.*

'I just love this old record, Sis, *Get on down* by Gene Chandler. Remember when we were young; we used to boogie to Sister Sledge, K.C. and the Sunshine Band, Sylvester and Sly and Robbie. Those were the days,' Lydia sighs, swaying her childbearing hips.

With drinks in hand we do an old shuffle, giggling and singing while imitating our mother trying to hook the latest moves. Mum loves Greek folk dances. She always throws a bit of "that" in to add flavour to what she calls the "Mediterranean mood".

'Hey, Sis, let's have another drink, one for that slimy bastard's future broken knuckles. His hands are going to be pigmy-size if he slaps my chocolate muffin one more time.'

'Yeah, I'm with you. You need to supplement the down time at the office, this will set you free.'

I pass Lydia a relaxed looking glass with a red tinsel umbrella covering its upper body. The bottle of rum stands half full, I only bought it this morning to celebrate Mum's sixtieth birthday. I hate rum usually, but I wanted Mum to have a little taste of home. She normally doesn't drink at the best of times. But we, her daughters, made a pact to gang-up on her to taste the devil's brew, hoping to ease the starch from her collar.

'I have to hand it to you, Lyd, you've got good taste in music.'

The South American white rum is sweet like coconut milk and deadly to dieting women. *POW* – straight to the back of the head. I'll probably wake-up with hairy nipples tomorrow.

'Sis, if that old, saggy arse mule comes a limping and a sniffing around my *mumf* once more, I'm telling ya, he's gonna fucking get it.'

Lyd balls a fist and twists her ankle in her high brown pumps, spilling blackcurrant punch on the white carpet. She bends down, trying to mop the stain with the Latin, pink sleeve of her blouse.

'Don't worry about it,' I said, pointing to the mark, 'You know, he'll get a clout from me too, that mucus-filled bald head. Give me your glass; it needs topping-up. We might as well finish the rest of the honey.'

I shake the last measure in the bottle like a maraca.

'Let's do the limbo, Sis.'

'Yeah. Let's sing. *And the beat goes on. We've got the funk, we've got the funk yeah.*'

We sing woozy, sharp tunes while walking on our bottoms.

The Gold Tessera

It is the third Sunday in June 2017, the temperature is scorching, 41°C. I'm in the historical Italian city, Ravenna. Accompanying on a pilgrimage, a seventy-five-year-old relative, Uncle Nathan. This is my first visit. Over the years, Uncle has been here several times. Our destination is the *Basilica of San Vitale*, an octagonal designed church.

Uncle Nathan is bubbling with excitement. As the church comes into view, his steps quicken. He's agile even though he uses an elaborate walking cane with a black ivory grip to aid him.

About fifty metres from the church's entrance, he says in an excited tone of a school boy, 'This is one of the most significant examples of Christian Byzantine art; it's glorious. The gold and the light are marvels.'

'You don't say?' There's a hint of sarcasm in my reply, eyes roll.

Once in the building, we walk ever so slowly so that Uncle can feast his eyes on the opulent mosaics.

The old man turns to face me, 'It's such a shame you must keep on your sunglasses.'

'I'm fine. What I've heard about gold holds no interest for me.'

'Suit yourself, my eyes will sup on the divine delights,' Uncle Nathan huffs, and leaves.

I sit in a pew. A family of five are also sitting there. Two of the children are laughing and pointing at me, I guess because of my dark glasses. I try to ignore them and look upwards to the lunettes above the triforia where a series of mosaics portray sacrifices from the Old Testament. After a few minutes, my neck aches. I cast my eyes to the ground as something near my left trainer catches my attention. I pick it up, it's a tessera; a small cube. The object sits in my palm, I gaze at it. On one side, the cube is painted. I know its gold as I read it in a guidebook.

The clicking sound of Uncle's cane comes closer.

'What have you there?'

'A tessera. It must have come loose from the wall.'

'How marvellous, let me see.'

Uncle Nathan sits beside me and inspects the gold glass cube. 'A wonderful piece of craftsmanship, don't you think?'

I shrug my shoulders. 'It reminds me of a cell.'

'A what!'

'A cell,' I nod. 'Yes, a prison cell.'

'You can't see the tessera clearly, Ethan,' Uncle lifts the cube to eye level, he licks his top lip. 'But this side is painted gold.' He draws out the last word, gold.

'A fool's colour.'

'Not for the early Christians. While worshipping, they must've thought they were looking straight at heaven, paradise.'

'Huh, I don't know about that.'

'Think, tens of thousands of gold tesserae are on this wall alone. They catch the light in the church like lenses. It's not the dreary light of electricity, it's pure brilliance.'

'The basilica must have cost a fortune. And the city's poor citizens worked like slaves to create all this.' I raise my arms high and then let them flop to my lap.

'But, I'm sorry, don't you think it was worth a few sacrifices? This will be admired through the ages. It's an UNESCO protected building.'

'Unfortunately, the dead can't speak. If they had a choice, I'm sure they'd have opted to worship under the sun in the shade of a large handsome tree.'

Uncle Nathan raises his voice, it echoes around the church, 'Outdoors is not the same.'

'Why not? Gold is the colour of the sun, but the sun is an actual heavenly body. And it's free, you don't have to pay tithes or shove paper bills in that rotten box at the entrance.'

The caretaker of the church walks towards us down the aisle. His eyes appear dead. Lines on his face are rivetted like the edges of coins. His wrinkles came not from joy, I'm certain of this.

Uncle holds his hand over his mouth and whispers, 'We ought to give the tessera to him. He'll make sure it's restored to its rightful place.'

'That artificial kingdom of heaven.' I point to the large mosaic above us.

'Ethan, you shouldn't say such things.'

'I will throw the tessera into the nearest river.'

'Why?'

'I like the thought of the glass splintering like grains of sand. The gold will sink to the riverbed. That's where it belongs, back in the earth.'

'You wouldn't say such awful things if you didn't suffer from protoporphyria. I'm sorry for you. The disorder dampens your appreciation of exquisite things.'

'You shouldn't be. Being allergic to natural and artificial light enables me to see outside the cell and even this gold tessera.'

'I know the disorder runs through my side of the family. I'm sorry you inherited the bad gene from your Grandpa.'

'It's okay, Uncle. Going to school was rough. Some kids bullied me, it toughened me up though.'

I throw the cube into the air and then stash it away in a pocket of my jeans, but not for keeps.

Shuttle Frost

It's cold in here, thought Diane. *Too many books are upside down and there's a frowzy odour hanging like dust, covering everything. Even the fly's eggs on the lampshade are protected. The chair looks comfortable enough, but it is a home for moths and cat's fur. The old springs roll and unroll. My black coat has started to grow peroxide strawberry tufts around the collar. I hate cats.*

'I have this ache,' Diane said to Dr Morris, pressing a hand near her heart. She paused, wiping her eyes.

'How is it that you, doctors of "this and that" can fly people around the moon, mix genes together to produce a hairless rat with pig's ears, take soya beans and get them to taste like beef, but a weak womb has to go it alone, like a shopping bag with too many bottles in it. They say it has something to do with gravity.'

Diane's words whizzed along like they were on a roller coaster. Dr Morris nodded slowly, as if he had also experienced multiple miscarriages. He wore thick glasses.

She wondered about the darkness of the room and his eyes.

'My sisters first appeared when my husband left with Shuttle Frost in his neck, wearing an "excuse me" dark suit. They started to talk to me when I washed my hair. I bought dolls, which I sewed onto my clothes, so that they could feel me breathing. They enjoyed tasting my favourite foods.

'I love a good fried breakfast. My mother warned me about that, saying, *There is far too much cholesterol in that food. It is not good for the heart and it's definitely too heavy for the mind.* She blames cholesterol for my condition. Do you think it has something to do with it? Apparently, I'm thirty-two kilos overweight. The scales lied. I don't believe I am obese. I was sad on that day. It wanted to get on my case like the rest of them.'

Diane clenched a fist and then pointed a pudgy finger towards the window where a cat yawned.

Dr Morris pursed his lips. 'What do you think, Diane?' He asked. 'Do your eating disorders influence your condition?'

Diane shrugged her shoulders. A sudden pain crossed her face. She left the practice with red eyes.

Diane revealed some of her thoughts to Mary who worked at the bakery opposite the bus station. Diane always ordered a snack, three buttered croissants, and a mug of coffee with four spoons of sugar. Mary told her she should try sweeteners, but she refused.

'I'm trying to stay sweet under the skin for old Shuttle Frost,' said Diane.

'Who's old Shuttle Frost?'

'Dan, my ex who left me.'

'Oh! So, is he still in the picture then?'

'I hope so, but he's hanging out to dry somewhere under the carpet.'

'Aha, I understand,' said Mary.

Mary did not understand, but she did not want to look disinterested. Mary was fascinated by Diane, as she aired her thoughts. Mary tried to decipher them while taking orders.

Diane would remove her shoes outside the bakery and walk home barefoot.

Three months earlier, her husband had removed all the carpets from the apartment, but left the tacks on the floor that supported them. Thin wooden strips remained, vicious spikes framing the rooms. When she was not careful, the tacks pierced the soles of her feet as she walked, leaving bloody footprints.

'They wriggle like dolphins on a chain of glass beads, which I try to break. Once the chain is broken, I run as fast as I can to another corner of the room. Massaging my scalp causes another bead to plop from the chain. The next thing I try to do is to pull the cord on the side of the heavy curtains. I need to see the light and breathe fresh air, but the sisters always call out saying, *Please leave the inside air where it is, otherwise we'll die.* Then they pull me and kick me. They carry me from one to the other, adding lead to my weight. I feel vertigo drunk as I try to get up. They form a cart. It rolls me to the middle of a tepee.'

'Hmm, interesting,' Dr Morris said, while jotting down notes. 'Do you feel safe in the tepee?'

'No.' Tears rolled down the tip of Diane's nose, then to her chin.

Dr Morris fidgeted in his leather armchair. He checked the clock.

Diane looked at a window where a Persian cat sat. She stuck out her tongue and then grinned sarcastically at it. She mouthed the words *fuck you.*

'The yellow tissues on the table remind me of the daisies on my balcony, which I love to prune and water in the sun. Once I gave each of my sisters a doll and a flowerpot, but they threw the dolls on the sidewalk, and cut the flowers. They planted black nightshades in the earth to kill my fingernails. I gathered my plastic babies, put them in a basket and covered them with a blanket.'

'Do you remember to take your medicine daily, Diane? It's very important.'

'Why?'

'Because it helps with anxiety and disorganised thoughts.'

'Do I have disorganised thoughts?'

'You are experiencing severe problems.'

On her way to Dr Morris's practice, she would walk as close to the buildings as possible so that the sisters would not hail a taxi home or push her to run for a bus. Sometimes they would press her down so hard that the air seemed five inches above her head. She would walk with bulging eyes and a gaping mouth, striding across the bus station.

As she walked down the street to Dr Morris's office, she held on to one of the trees that lined the street. The autumn weather attacked her from all sides, sweeping up a storm of leaves. The leaves swirled around her waistline. Perhaps a soft word would make the remaining three hundred metres bearable. She stood thinking, *why can't you all just piss-off. I'm tired.*

At Dr Morris's practice, she blurted apologies for being late.

'Last night those Belladonnas bit the soles of my feet, God help me!' Diane said, prodding the weight around her waist with a twig. 'It stung like ten jealous hornets, and one of them had the audacity to slink into the room, wearing my wedding dress, with a tiara around her curls. I could smell my Dan's favourite perfume, *Choice,* as she held a freshly cut bouquet of daisies. I saw her splashing honey milk on her face, sneering.

'Then an army of hornets moved in and we slapped the air, but we got tired. My sisters fell into cocoons where they peeped through barred windows while the room circled. I tried to pick them up one by one, but they were too heavy. You see, Dr Morris, they need love too. We cried and rolled together like a family. I said *goodbye.*

'I slept and shook tight in the arms of old Shuttle Frost. He still wore his "excuse me" dark suit in the middle of the night. In the morning I could see mist above the balcony where four sweet caryatides were made from ice. The black nightshades had gone underground. One daisy head swayed to a lullaby sung by my neighbour Lindsay to comfort her child. I feel light now without any shopping, and Shuttle Frost seems to enjoy the scent of my skin. At least he has taken off his jacket.'

'It's almost time for you to leave,' said Dr Morris. 'Don't be too hard on yourself, as you're making fine progress. Take one step at a time. Remember to take your medicine and record any side effects.'

'I will.'

'Very good,' said Dr Morris. He smiled as he opened the door.

Diane dipped her aching feet into the outside world.

At home behind drawn curtains, Diane moved slowly around the kitchen.

She made two sandwiches, swollen with cheese, ham and egg. The black sandwich toaster sat open on the white counter with a sneering, rotten mouth. Diane could not wait to close it, using all of her strength until she heard the lid click into place.

A minute later, melted cheese and egg sizzles, and seeps out making tiny yellow pools. She smears some with a finger, closes her eyes and tastes. The green light flashes on. A knife and fork rest on a plate as if eagerly open.

The World in an Eye

Daniel walks the muddy tracks to school from his khaki waterproof home to the caravan where the orphans learn to read, write, and draw camouflaged Leopard 1 tanks and M16 rifles the same colour as the mud.

'Have you found me a mummy or pappy yet?' He asks his teacher.

'Sorry, Daniel, this time is not your time. Mr. and Mrs. Roland want a girl. Look, Sharon is crying because she must leave Issy behind, her two-year-old sister.'

Issy's body is balled in a cupboard under the sink. She is sucking her thumb as if it were a whole world of sugar.

Not too far in the distance, a motor changes several gears. The cream Volvo is stuck in the mud. The mud is splashing its metal carcass, just like the barrage of bullets Daniel had heard, cracking the air, and splitting his mother's brow. He watched her falling from the tips of her toes to the soft ground where the mud kissed his shoes. Slowly the mud dried and cracked like a beauty pack from the Dead Sea.

'Go along, Daniel,' his mother whispered, 'I'm just going to rest here for a while.'

A tear caressed the side of her cheek as she expelled a puff of breath, which lived longer than she did. Higher and higher the little curl of steam rose, then disappeared out of reach on the road where angels tread. It was the first and last time that Daniel appreciated the mud, the way it held his mother, moulding to her form like an orthopaedic bed, letting her sleep in cushioned comfort. He hoped for ever.

Medecins sans Frontiers nursed his bullet scratch on the left eye and wrapped his mother like half a pound of Edam in a dreary, old oilskin sheet.

Daniel does not remember exactly when he became an orphan or how old he is. The numbness set in when his twin brother Tommy died. Tommy took with him the sun, the tears, and the fear that used to strangle them both as they hid in old cupboards in derelict houses. They hoped the sound of the chewing woodworm would not give them away, but Daniel thought they did because a grenade fell and blew open Tommy's cupboard like the gaping jaws of hell. Daniel could not identify his brother. Blood, wood, and mortar were everywhere. There was not even a bucket of sticky mud to preserve his brother's face. At that point, the hate for the mud moved in.

Daniel hates the caravan. The wheels sink down as if to the earth's crust, never once turning. The musty odour of patience sitting within the children's clothes, and the toilet that made the mud even muddier. In single file children with old eyes walk silently through the door and spring into the muddy world where the sky had splintered and cracked, leaking driving rain. They say goodbye to Sharon with sullen drenched faces.

Sharon strokes her sister's soggy hair; a kiss would hurt too much. *America*, she thinks as she climbs into the tainted Volvo without looking back, *the land of milk and honey.*

Daniel looks around the camp between curtains of rain, where orphans had morbidly painted on every tent except the lazaret. The paintings depicted skeleton armies advancing without mercy, stomping over the sun, trees, and over bodies. Only four colours were used in the pictures: red, white, grey, and black. Each victim's initials was boldly capitalised in red. There were ferocious animals eating flesh. It was a bizarre picture similar to the horrifying one in the Bible where Pharaoh commands "every boy that is born" to be thrown into the Nile which was infested with crocodiles. This prehistoric animal was still very much alive in Europe, a long way from home on metallic revolving feet. Its spirit churned in the *Leopard 1* tanks that were now burning and changing the face of land to muddy swamps. Only the fortunate were able to escape to concrete valleys and Sharon was one of them.

There is no mud except in the graphite clouds passing above Sharon's window frame. They remind her of the tents, tanks, drawings of school friends, and the sister she left behind crawling in the uncertain light.

Niesha's Blackened Lips

Polio has seized my body. I move through a crowded street. Eyes shun me and legs run to hide. The street holds me in dust, as I wait for the rush to die. My arms, work like legs, bearing the muscles of a warrior, deftly walking me down the streets. Hands are deformed. They are not the hands of a woman or a beast. Loneliness grips at the heart; it is sore from being clawed.

The sun has bled heat over me, blackening my lips. This unwashed face wears only tears. Salt burns my weathered skin; blisters open like sad eyes and weep. They weep for my dead family and for me. What are my hopes today, a piece of chapatti, or a bowl of rice?

Three years before the rains fell hard. We tried to save our homes, but the wetness would not drain away. We gathered diseases from stagnant pools of water. Bodies sunk into the surging deep. We could not help but trample over love, as we needed to drink the rain.

Rain carried away the *charpoy* my child slept in. His father left the next morning with fever, in search of his small son. I watched him from a neighbour's rooftop, flailing in the torrent. I never saw him again.

I rest on precarious stone steps, bound to a board. Rags hold my snake-like skin. The grimy tarlatan folds I wear are of no comfort to a woman. I would love some oil to loosen the leathery hold and a silk sari where the walk and scent of a woman flourishes. I used to stand naked in the deep of night with jasmine oil coating the air, imagining my husband's silhouette under moonlight. We moved as one. It was the only way to feel him long after he had gone to work in the city. Sometimes I did not see him for days, but even then, I felt like a woman.

He always whispered, 'I love all your sacred jewels.'

I am still a woman, who feels like a woman and endures pain like a woman. I have given birth to life, bearing those scars of a woman. I used to have rosebud lips, but the sun entered them and robbed the beauty.

A man passed me this morning, shouting, 'Swamp monster, get out of the way!' He spat on the ground.

By accident, my right palm trod in his slimy anger. I prayed, *Moon, paint a light coffin over a grassy plane, I will gladly crawl into it. Please darken the night. Let the stars dim under a sable veil, so I can milk the earth to feel full again. Open earth's heart, so the tears of a weeping soul can seep into the soil and blossom like a lotus in a dream.*

I have started to practise *Jyâna* yoga; Jyâna in Sanskrit means "knowledge". It allows me to see outside this world, to delight, and be glad in the *self*. In this state, I am free, no longer a prisoner of a putrid body, crippled by paralysis. This is only a temporal state.

A bruised fruit lies on a step. I roll it over an aged cheek while whispering a verse from the *Bhagavad-Gita*, 'The soul can never be cut into pieces by any weapon, nor can he be burned by fire, nor moistened by water, nor withered by the wind.'

So, in the light of an awakening day, I will always be seen as a woman in the essence of the earth. And I will pretend my blackened lips are rosebuds to exorcise the darkness to light.

The Double Bass

Derek cried uncontrollably as his father lay heaving for breath under the oxygen mask. A seizure had taken hold again. He had so many epileptic fits since suffering a stroke eighteen months ago and had a tracheostomy tube inserted in the neck. Five minutes struggled by in the summer-heated hospital room. I felt trapped. I just wanted to run, run far away, deep into the park across the street where the water from the lake soothes. Soon, it was over, the long haul of minutes.

The pain ceased. The old man's head flopped to the side where his mouth leaked a slither of saliva onto the pillowcase.

Derek stroked the lifeless head; his lips moved, but I heard nothing. I think he was whispering a prayer. We siblings stood holding each other for a while, as nurses moved solemnly towards the bed. They wheeled it out of the room, pushed it down the dimly lit hallway to the old lift that took the now peaceful sleeper to the end station; the basement where the lifeless are covered up and housed.

At home, Derek was struck by a force of numbness that wracked his body. I put on an old Louis Armstrong CD that our father used to love. I turned the volume up, almost to the ten. The song's words hovered in the space below the ceiling. Smiling, laughing people came like friendly ghosts to mind, trying to tease us back to the land of living.

Derek walked to the corner of the room where our father's double bass stood in a black soft padded case with two small wheels at the base. He pushed the bass, and stopped in front of the Essex upright piano, as I sat, cross-legged on the rosewood stool. Derek unzipped the bag, removed the bass, and rested its round maple back against his body. He hit the D-string with a thumb and then reached for the bow, which was in a leather quiver near the bottom of the instrument. Derek held the black horsehair bow with an underhand grip. He sent the bow rushing across the five strings with such force, the bass screeched.

I shuddered as the vibrations ran up my legs. Derek took out a cake of rosin from a small pocket of the case; gently he applied the balm to the bow. Some snagged hairs rose in the air, wisps swayed in the fake breeze circulated by the electric fan. The wayward hairs smoothed into a neat black strip. The bow glided over the strings; the action looked beautiful.

'Dez, it's going to be all right,' I said.

He continued playing, the sound became lighter, the stroke tender. Blue raspy vocals melted with bass tones. Tears splashed polished wood.

'Dad's gone to a better place, Dez, you know. He's with Mum, now.' I swallowed a huge invisible lump that felt as if it sat on top of my larynx.

'I know, Cory, it's just that we never finished the tune we were working on, *Close To You*. Dad wrote it for Mum a while back. He missed her so much, me too.'

'You shouldn't have given up. Mum and Dad would've loved you to keep on playing.'

'I was bored of practising. It's a shame because I don't know where that song sheet is now.'

I would have given anything to spend some musical time with Dad. He was such a talented multi-instrumentalist; a great mentor for any child. Unfortunately, due to years of illness and ear infections when young, my hearing became impaired. Airways were forever blocked and my eardrums had to be perforated several times. I became too frail to hold the double bass.

I was jealous of Derek back then, being so fond of the bass vibrations coming up from the wooden floor, they teased my body. I truly heard the music; every tone lived in me and petered out over the skin. Dad bought me the best hearing aids, very sensitive; they picked up a lot.

I learnt to lip read as well. It helps to get through the day. I do so love listening, feeling and creating music from within. I know every word, every nuance of Mum's song. The melodies and harmonies lift my spirit. I sung the words over a hundred times in my head accompanied by a complete orchestra on the day of her funeral.

'Yes, you're right,' Derek said with one hand on the hip of his baggy jeans. More tears splashed his apple-green shirt.

'Look, it's all still here, the instruments, the CDs, records, music sheets. Dad's within every note. You'll see. He'll guide you.'

'Do you think I could become as good as him?'

'There's no harm in trying. The sheet music for Mum's song is under the fan.'

'Great. Do you know where Dad's repertoire is stored? Also, I'd like to get in touch with David, the pianist. I don't know where he lives. His flat's uptown somewhere.'

'The address is in Dad's notebook.'

I stood to lift the burgundy leather top of the piano stool and waded through papers. The notebook sat on top of the pile.

I waved it above my head., 'Look here. I have a list and a map. What could possibly go wrong? You have everything you need to get started.'

'Thanks, Cory. You're a great sister!'

'You just go ahead. I'll fry up some plantains and prepare a nice bit of jerk chicken and rice just like Mum used to cook back in the days on a Sunday, as you jammed with Dad. You'll soon get the swing of it.'

In the kitchen, my mind wandered back to my eleventh birthday where I received the number one gift from my parents. They gave me a huge gift-wrapped present. I knew what it was – my dream. With no time to waste, I tore off the wrapping so fast it floated above me. A picture of my favourite instrument stood printed on the carton.

'Awesome, a bass, just what I wanted. Thanks so much.'

I ran to hug Mum and Dad. They beamed. Mum had tears in her eyes. I did too. 'It's a kit,' said Dad. 'A plywood student bass, a cover, bow and rosin.'

Dad helped to unpack the half-size instrument and showed me how to use an underhand grip on the bow. My first lesson was magical.

'This instrument is tuned in fourths not fifths like a violin and cello.'

'Okay.'

The first song I learned to play was *Little Brown Jug* written in 1869 by Joseph Winner. At the age of twelve, I played the tune in public for the first time at a party my parents threw. They were celebrating their fifteenth wedding anniversary. Dad accompanied me on the piano. After playing, everyone rose to their feet, shouting, 'Bravo, bravo...'

I thought the applause would never end. There wasn't a dry eye in sight. The memory still leaves me tingling. It causes me to smile and cry at the same time.

Unusual Talk in a Foreign Land

Berlin 2019

The heat is killing me. I'm in Germany for goodness sake, I can't believe the temperature is 34°C. The soles of my feet are aching and I'm worn through. Peace and tranquillity are needs.

So, here I am, minding my own business, sitting on sun-warmed concrete slab steps with splashes of duck droppings in front of the *Schloss Charlottenburg's* picturesque lake. The garrulous ducks, thrushes and swans snap and squabble over a large piece of bread thrown from a toddler's smudgy hand. The little mite shrieks with a bird-like tone.

I rummage through my large bag for a poetry anthology. Because of the boisterousness, it's difficult to concentrate on verse, so I read softly to myself. I enjoy the rhythm of words sounding against the backdrop of chatter.

A young man's effeminate voice filters through, 'Turn around, stop vogueing. Just give me one pose, not ten.' The man's chuckle is infectious.

I look up and say, smiling, 'Leave her alone, the lady wants to be her best. Oh, that's a nice pose, keep it, smile.'

The attractive woman's sable-skinned face is turned towards us. Her chin rests on the petite knuckles of her clenched left hand.

The photographer tuts. 'There's nothing but pressure,' the young man says. 'Where are you from anyway?'

He looks towards me and then drops his hand with the camera to his right side. He smirks, but his eyes hold another story from the niceties of the day.

'I'm from England.'

'Ah, yes, that counts.'

'Where are you from?'

His answer pierces my mind. 'Trust the people to colonise you and then forget to recognise you.'

'What? That's an interesting, but strange answer. But you can't say that to a person of colour, to me.'

'It was a bad joke. I'm from Ghana.'

'As the saying goes, *there's no smoke without fire.*'

He raises his voice as he shifts, taking a rigid stance, 'I told you, it was a bad joke.'

'Okay, okay, I hear you. Are you learning German in the city?'

'Yes, I'm staying around the corner.'

'Oh, me too. Which road do you live in?'

'Bremen.'

'You're a funny one, aren't you? That's quite a distance away from here, I think it's over 300 kilometres or so.'

I turn smiling to the young woman, who has been listening to our strange interaction, saying, 'You have a lot to handle with this one, yes?'

With a sweet motion, my eyes flit on her friend. He's fretting, scuffing the ground with his shoes.

'Correct,' she pats her friend's arm in a soothing manner.

I sense the touch holds a world of compassion and understanding. There is a depth to this friendship that a stranger cannot fathom.

She continues, 'I'm learning German too. And...'

The young man motions to a large group, 'We've got to get back to our friends. We met them last week at the *Christopher Street Day Festival.*'

On the other side of the expansive steps, a party of vividly dressed young people sit. The men are dressed in the hues of birds of paradise. Two light-skinned men exchange featherlike almost casual touches. They are drinking red wine from plastic cups and eating crisps the same colour as the vibrant sun. The group appear unburdened, living to the full.

My eyes regain their focus, back on to the two people beside me.

The young man hunches as I say, 'Ah, yes, I read about that day in the local paper. It was sometime last week, I think.'

The young woman, giddy with excitement adds, 'I love the LGBT parades with all their eye-catching floats and pumping music. The sounds and colours are super and it was fab to see so many having a good time and celebrating a valid cause too. I danced for hours to Techno. It was just like a rave.'

The photographer cuts in with, 'My land is not tolerant. We can't express ourselves; gays must hide. Live under the cover of darkness.'

'Oh, that's a shame. I wish you both all the best. And you,' my index finger points to the young man, I whisper, 'you have something in your head.'

I nod and wink. The young Ghanaian beams and straightens his handsome long neck.

I'm happy he's got my meaning: *you're special.* For a few seconds, the three of us share common ground and genuine smiles.

Glossary

Dripping Teeth

Halitosis
Bad breath.

Uvula
A small fleshy finger-like flap of tissue that hangs in the back of the throat and is an extension of the soft palate.

Looking for Polly

iPhone
A type of mobile phone which includes a music player and internet browser.

We Owe It to You

Rosa Parks
Rosa Parks (born Rosa Louise McCauley Parks on 4th February 1913, passed away on 24th October 2005) was an American activist in the civil rights movement best known for her pivotal role in the Montgomery bus boycott. The United States Congress has called her "the first lady of civil rights" and "the mother of the freedom movement".

Punch Drunk

Mumf

(A neologism, commonly known as made up word) backside, behind, buttocks, posterior, bum.

The Gold Tessera

Tessera

A small block of stone, tile, glass, or other material used in the construction of a mosaic.

Protoporphyria

The result of having too much Porphyrin causes allergic reactions to light, both natural and artificial.

Shuttle Frost

Black Nightshade

A poisonous solanaceous plant, Solanum nigrum, a common weed in cultivated land, having small white flowers with backward-curved petals and black berry-like fruits.

Dead Sea

A salt lake about 50 miles (80 kilometres) long on the boundary between Israel and Jordan, area 370 square miles (962 square kilometres).

Note: The Dead Sea contains the lowest point on the Earth's surface. Its surface is 1312 feet (400 meters) below sea level.

The uncommonly temperate, extremely buoyant and mineral-rich waters have drawn visitors since antiquity, including King Herod the Great and the exquisite Egyptian Queen, Cleopatra.

Medecins sans Frontiers (MSF)

Also written in English as *Doctors Without Borders*, is an international humanitarian medical non-governmental organisation (NGO) of French origin best known for its projects in conflict zones and in countries affected by endemic diseases.

The Leopard (or Leopard 1)

A main battle tank designed and produced by Porsche in West Germany that first entered service in 1965.

Lazaret

1. A hospital treating contagious diseases.
2. A building or ship used as a quarantine station.

Charpoy
A bed used especially in India consisting of a frame strung with tapes or light rope.

Jyâna Yoga or "path of knowledge"
One of the types of yoga mentioned in Hindu philosophies.

Bhagavad-Gita
A sacred Hindu text that is incorporated into the Mahabharata and takes the form of a philosophical dialogue in which Krishna instructs the prince Arjuna in ethical matters and the nature of God.

The Double Bass

Tracheostomy
A hole that surgeons make through the front of the neck and into the windpipe (trachea). A tracheostomy tube is placed into the hole to keep it open for breathing. The term for the surgical procedure to create this opening is tracheotomy.

Essex upright piano
Essex upright pianos benefit from the exclusive construction features and patents of Steinway & Sons.

Rosin
1. Also called: colophony: a translucent brittle amber substance produced in the distillation of crude turpentine oleoresin and used especially in making varnishes, printing inks, and sealing waxes and for treating the bows of stringed instruments.
2. (not in technical usage) another name for resin.

Unusual Talk in a Foreign Land

Schloss Charlottenburg (Charlottenburg Palace)
A Baroque palace in Berlin, located in Charlottenburg, a district of the Charlottenburg-Wilmersdorf borough.

The palace was built at the end of the 17th century and was greatly expanded during the 18th century. It includes much lavish internal decoration in baroque and rococo styles.

A large formal garden surrounded by woodland was added behind the palace, including a belvedere, a mausoleum, a theatre and a pavilion.

During the Second World War, the palace was badly damaged but has since been reconstructed. The palace with its gardens is a major tourist attraction.

Christopher Street Day Festival (CSD)
An annual European LGBT celebration and demonstration held in various cities across Europe for the rights of LGBT people and against discrimination

and exclusion. It is Germany's and Switzerland's counterpart to Gay Pride or Pride Parades.

Acknowledgements

The following stories have been previously published:

For the Love of Money: 2019 Sunlight (501©3 nonprofit digital journal), The Sunlight Press

The Papaya Stall: 2015 The Caribbean Writer, volume 29, University of the Virgin Islands

Dripping Teeth: 2015 Thrice Fiction magazine issue No.15, US

Waiting: 2013, Thrice Fiction magazine issue No.8, US

What's It All For?: 2012 Connections: an anthology of short stories, Paragram, UK

Niesha's Blackened Lips: 2012 – *Blood Orange*, M. Blades' poetry book, Erbacce Press, UK

The World in an Eye: 2011 World Selected Prose, The Smartest Kid in the Bronx Published, Latin Heritage Foundation, US

We Owe It to You – For Rosa Parks: 2005 Cornelsen Verlag, Ger.

Punch Drunk: 2004 *Das Buch Vom Trinken* anthology Verbrecher Verlag, Ger.

Also By Chapeltown Books

Theme and Varations
by Vanessa Horn

Theme and Variations is a collection of sixteen flash fiction stories with music – some of it harmonious, some discordant – running through them.

Although fictional, these stories also contain many elements of realism. After all, music will always be with, around or in you

Order from Amazon:

ISBN: 978-1-910542-51-4 (paperback)
978-1-910542-52-1 (ebook)

Chapeltown Books

140 x 140
by Gill James

This anthology of women's fiction, this collection of very short stories, some might say a flash collection, is thought-provoking and each story is based upon a tweet. Except that each piece is 140 words long and not 140 characters.

"In this entertaining book, Gill James chose the first picture she saw on her Twitter feed on specific dates. As the title suggests, there are 140 stories, each of 140 words. Some tales are laugh out loud funny, others thoughtful, and there are tragic stories too. Whatever your mood, you will find plenty to suit you here." *(Amazon)*

Order from Amazon:

ISBN: 978-1-910542-35-4 (paperback)
978-1-910542-36-1 (ebook)

Chapeltown Books

Paisley Shirt
by Gail Aldwin

Paisley Shirt is a fascinating collection of 27 stories that reveal the extraordinary nature of people and places. Through a variety of characters and voices, these stories lay bare the human experience and what it is like to live in our world.

"I really enjoyed every one of Gail Aldwin's perfectly-formed little stories, and was hooked from the very first one." (*Amazon*)

Order from Amazon:
ISBN: 978-1-910542-29-3 (paperback)
978-1-910542-30-9 (ebook)

Chapeltown Books

www.ingramcontent.com/pod-product-compliance
Lightning Source LLC
Chambersburg PA
CBHW080753120626
46557CB00005B/1255

* 9 7 8 1 9 1 0 5 4 2 5 6 9 *